For my best little buddy, Callie (and any
other grandchildren I may someday
have); with thanksgiving for Sandy
and so many others who have shared
encouragement; and with a grateful heart
to the Lord for His countless blessings.

![MASCOT KIDS!]

**www.mascotbooks.com**

*Good Brother No*

©2021 David G. Oravec. All Rights Reserved. No part of this publication may be reproduced, stored in a retrieval system or transmitted in any form by any means electronic, mechanical, or photocopying, recording or otherwise without the permission of the author.

**For more information, please contact:**
Mascot Books
620 Herndon Parkway, Suite 320
Herndon, VA 20170
info@mascotbooks.com

Library of Congress Control Number: 2021911192

CPSIA Code: PRT0721A

ISBN-13: 978-1-64543-963-9

Printed in the United States

# GOOD BROTHER NO

Pastor Dave Oravec

Illustrated by
Lucian Gradinariu

A long time ago, in a land far away,
there once was a time, there once was a day
when people were bad—yes, really quite rotten.
Though God gave them all, they'd quickly forgotten.
They were ugly and nasty and lousy and mean.
They did nothing but evil—a horrible scene!

Now, the Good Lord looked down, and He scratched His big head.
*Hmmm, what to do?* He thought, and He said,
"I could just let them go, but don't think that I should—
I made them to LOVE, and I wish that they would."

God tried, and He tried, but they paid Him no mind.
They laughed, and they mocked Him—they were very unkind.

Then, God decided on one fateful day,
"No more of this nonsense. I'll wash them away.
I'm sorry I made them; they cause so much woe.
All except one . . .

. . . That Good Brother No!"
No's full name was Noah, and he understood
the reason God made him was to love and do good.
So Noah found favor in the eyes of the Lord.
He worshipped and praised Him; yes, God he adored.

It was soon after that that God came and said,
"No, pay attention—get up out of bed.
Please listen closely; I've something to say.
It's soon going to rain, get started today.
Go build you a boat, and make sure it will float.
I'll tell you how, so listen—take note."
So Brother No listened, and God told him how
to build a huge boat, then said, "Build it—now!"

So, off Noah went to cut down some wood.
He sharpened his ax—he sharpened it good.
He cut hundreds of trees. He used leaves, he used bark,
and he made a big ship, which he called . . .

# NOAH'S ARK!

Then, God spoke again, saying, "Fill up the boat with two of each creature." It put a lump in No's throat. There was so much to do, it made Noah dizzy. "I'd better get started! I'd better get busy!"

So, Brother No went
throughout all the land
for the boy and girl critters
each made by God's hand.

Grasshoppers, zebras, rhinos, and bears; elephants, tigers, and bouncy brown hares.

There were pigs and giraffes and emus and frogs;
lions and snakes and, of course, Noah's dogs.
Some didn't listen, but some came with ease.
No had no trouble convincing the fleas!

So, slowly but surely, the ark he did fill.
And for just a few moments, it was quiet and still,
and everyone listened, from the flea to the crane.
And then they all heard it . . . it started to rain.
It started out slowly—a pitter-pat-pit—
but Brother No knew that this was now it.

Yes, this was the rain that Almighty God sent.
And then it came down like the heavens were rent!
It rained and it rained, all night and all day;
the flood waters grew—they swept evil away.

It rained, and it rained, and the flood waters rose,
and the only ones left were those God had chose:
two of each creature, No, and his clan.
But this was the way a new beginning began.
For after the Lord had poured out His wrath
and given the earth a much-needed bath,
He rethought it all, and then came to say,
"I'll do this no more. I'll find a new way."

So, the raindrops stopped falling; the ark floated around,
and No began thinking he'd soon see dry ground.
He looked and he looked, but all that he spied
was water and water—his patience was tried.
So he planned, and he thought; he thought, and he planned
about a good way to discover dry land.
And then it hit him, like a bolt from above.
"I know!" cried Noah. "I'll send out a dove."

So, out went the dove from the big floating zoo.
And she brought back a branch, and then Noah knew
that the ride was soon over; they'd be done with the ark.
Yes, he and the animals could soon disembark.

And so, the day came the Lord spoke like before:
"It's time to get out, No. Open the door."

So, the big hatch was opened, and oh! What a sight!
The dirt and the rocks and the sun shining bright.
Now the earth looked so different—so clean and so new—
and the critters came off the ark two by two.

They all were so happy. They ran, and they played.
But, Good Brother No, he knelt down, and he prayed.
He offered his praise to the Good Lord above;
he thanked Him for life and His unending love.
And God was delighted with Good Brother No,
and He promised to bless him and his offspring also.

He promised He'd never again send a flood.
In fact, He would sooner shed His own blood
than destroy all the people, despite their cruel sin.
He'd make a new way; He vowed to begin.

He'd make a new way to wash sin away
while saving the sinner—we know it today!

And just to remind us, like Good Brother No,
we still, on occasion, see a heavenly show.
Up in the sky as we're walking along,
the beautiful colors, like a beautiful song.
Streaking across the heavens above,
reminding us still of His marvelous love.

Yes, just to remind us, like dear Brother No,
we behold the splendor of a brilliant rainbow.
It's almost as if God's hands leave a trace
while opening wide for a loving embrace!

So, here ends the story, my friends, as you see.
And though it's of Noah—it's about you and me.
About each child of God and His great gift of grace.
May His love fill your heart and shine on your face!